The Train

Jack Preston

The Train

Cover Design: Ken Preston

Contents

The Train

Chapter One
The Plans

"Name?"

"C. Daniel."

"Thank you."

It was Victorian times, in a snow covered hotel, London. It was the joyous and wonderful time of the year called Christmas, and as you looked around you could see oil lamps attached to metal poles covered in snow, whilst smartly dressed men tipped their hats at passers by and vice versa. Inside the large, rectangular building known as The Arlingnton Hotel, two men outside pushed the door open letting a rush of cold air into the warm building. They went up to the reception desk, checked in and then went into the restaurant for a meal of pan roasted duck breasts with raspberry sauce.

"Do you have it?" said C. Daniel, sitting down in his seat.

"Yes," said his work partner Raymond, picking up his napkin he had just accidentally knocked onto the floor.

"So the plan is going ahead, then?"

"Yes, yes it is. Everything has gone to plan as expected."

"Erm… the papers please?"

"Oh yes, sorry about that. Here they are."

Raymond produced a bunch of papers stapled together and slid them across the table to Daniel. The papers had three letters printed at the top of the front page, C.M.C. As Daniel flipped through the pages, he nodded and sometimes even smiled. But it wasn't a pleasant smile. It was a smile that would put you off your food, a smile that would make you want to run as far away as possible. It was an evil smile.

"When is the plan going to be put into action?" he asked, as the waiter arrived with their starters.

"Saturday the twenty-fourth."

"Ah, Christmas Eve, a good choice."

"Thank you, I decided on that."

"Anyway, who is the train going to stop for?"

"Erm…" Raymond had turned around and was watching a mysterious looking man dressed all in black pour a liquid around the outside of the hotel.

"Raymond!" Daniel shouted. "Who is going on the train?"

"Sca—" Raymond stopped mid-sentence because of what he saw at the side of the building.

Flames.

Lots of them.

He glanced around the room and noticed that people had already seen. Several of them had got up and were running for the door, whilst others grabbed the nearest fire extinguishers and attempted to put out the flames.

Raymond grabbed the papers and ran out, not knowing if C. Daniel was okay. He stood for a moment on the thick red carpet in the main lobby, not knowing what to do. A door at the back caught his eye. Without thinking, he pushed through the hectic crowd of shouts and screams, and straight down into the wine cellar.

Phew, he thought to himself. *I'll be safe down here. I'd better check the door though to make sure I can get out when the fire has gone down.*

He ran back up and twisted then pulled the handle. Locked.

He shot back down. He needed to protect the all-important papers. He started to heftily haul some of the large crates of wine over the papers, to try and protect them from the fire.

At least the papers will be safe, he thought to himself.

He went back up the stairs. It was worth a shot banging on the door to grab someone's attention. He started to bang loudly and scream, but nobody heard. They were all outside, safe and sound. He stopped and rested his head against the door for a moment. It felt different than before, much warmer. His heart was thumping and his head was spinning with dizziness as he ran down the steps and pushed his body as far back as he could against the stone wall. Everything was a blur as he saw the fire crackle on the wooden floor above him, edging towards him, as he experienced his entire life flash before him in less than a second: he knew this was the end.

Nausea took over his body as he watched with terror as the fire came closer and closer towards him.

Outside, the people standing in the snow watching the hotel burn heard a deafening cry from within the flames.

The next day, Daniel was walking along the street. He turned into a large brick building and walked up to a burly, thuggish looking man who had been crammed into a suit that would probably burst if he ate just one more doughnut, who was standing on the door step.

"ID please?" the man said, nonchalantly.

"Here you are," replied C. Daniel, pulling out a small slip of paper and showing it to the man.

The man nodded.

C. Daniel walked in through two large doors and

into the meeting place of C.M.C. The room was very grand and a table stretched all the way down the room, past several pillars, which were holding up the balconies on either side of the room. There were several people sitting at the table, one of them being the head of the organisation, Scat Knight. Nobody knows where he was born, when he was born, who his parents are, or even why he is the head of the C.M.C. His entire life is a mystery.

Daniel sat down, trying desperately not to look at all the staring faces as he walked in the room without his work partner. He sat down, next to the Italian worker Giovanno and his work partner Ciara.

Scat took a sip of water from his glass and started talking.

"Hello Daniel, I heard your companion has died."

"Y-y-yes, boss," Daniel said nervously.

"So we don't need you anymore."

"Yes, boss., shall I leave then," Daniel said, starting to stand up.

Scat laughed quietly to himself. "Sit back down, sit back down. We can transport you outside a lot quicker than walking."

And with this Scat pressed a button on his desk, causing Daniel's chair to tip back to his death down a large, black hole.

London, The Cross Station, 7th of January 2017

On the rather famous train station, stood a boy with his Uncle Ur, in quite an awkward silence as a train pulled up onto the platform.

"Well, um, I guess I'll see you soon," said his uncle, breaking the silence.

"Yes. I… guess so." Thomas was in a silent ecstasy that he was finally leaving his horrible Uncle Ur.

"When are you gonna be back again?" said his uncle.

"I've already told you. Same time, next year."

He was living with his uncle as, a fair few years ago, Thomas' parents disappeared. They told him that they would be back soon, but never returned. After their disappearance (and a month later) they received a letter stating that Thomas' auntie and uncle had right to look after him. So they did.

Thomas didn't have much to pack to go to boarding school, because he didn't have very many possessions. He packed some clothes, a toothbrush and some toothpaste, some stationery (he'd promised to write to his auntie every week) and a Rubix cube for entertainment. He had messy hair, and a pair of glasses which sat at an odd angle on his face.

He wore normal clothes a teenage boy would wear, but didn't think himself much of an ordinary adolescence. Secretly he hated his uncle. He much preferred his auntie, but his uncle was awful. He constantly had a pair of trousers on which were too low down and he wore a T-shirt which was too small, so all his fat would hang out whenever he bent down.

"All aboard! Train departing in five minutes to Montpellier, France."

"Well, there's my stop." said Thomas.

"I'll see you soon."

"Um… yeah, see you soon."

Thomas walked over to the train and got on, not bothering to look back at the terror of his old life.

Chapter Two
Dead Pop

Thomas walked along the train carriages until he found an empty seat. He was sitting next to a girl, smartly dressed in a beret and a suit.

"Morning," said the girl, still staring out of the window.

"Actually, it's afternoon," replied Thomas, and this made the girl turn around to face him.

"Well," she said, "where are you going?"

"To France."

"No, I mean where abouts in France. I know you must be going to France because this train goes directly to Montpellier then back again. So?"

"I'm going to a boarding school."

"Is it called Montpellier Boarding School?"

Thomas felt like he was being interrogated with all these questions, but still he answered them all the same.

"Yeah, something like that."

"I'm going there as well."

"Are you? I'm glad I can go to this school so I

can have a break from working with my Uncle. Is it nice?"

"Just like any other school really. What was your Primary School's name?"

"I didn't go to one."

"Oh. Anyway, what's your name?"

"Thomas. What's yours?"

"Catherine Merillin. Or Cat for short."

"That's a bit of an odd name." Said Thomas, realising that must have been a bit rude to say.

"I know." She said, noticing Thomas' expression. "But it doesn't offend me. Everyone says it."

Thomas turned around to get his first good look at the carriage he was in. He hadn't realised how dirty it was. It was a grim and shabby place, a bit of a rubbish tip. All Thomas could hope for would be that the rooms were better. There was chewing gum underneath the chairs, sticking to anyone who dared touch it. The seats also were made out of a rough kind of fur, the kind you find being sold cheap at the Spittlefields Market. The walkways were littered with crisp packets, drink bottles and chocolate bar wrappers, and you could see some of the mechanisms sticking up underneath the chairs. It was the oldest train in London.

As Thomas' eyes were exploring the train, he heard a sudden noise. It sounded like a lever being pulled. He thought nothing of it then; yet it was going to change his entire life for him.

"Did you hear that?" Thomas said to Cat.

"No I did-" at that moment the lights went out and they were plunged into darkness.

"Damn lighting!" said someone from in the darkness, which was then followed by a series of banging noises and cursing. An ear-piercing scream came from one of the other carriages. The lights came back on and there were several other screams. People started to get up and move towards the carriage where all the noise had come from. Suddenly, someone gasped and fainted. Thomas and Cat stood up and pushed their way through the crowds.

At the place where everyone was, they couldn't see what they were looking at, because there were too many people in the way. Then, some one screamed at the top of their voice all the information they needed.

"Annie Red! She's dead!"

"Course she's gone an' dropped dead now." Someone muttered under his breath. "It was David Bowie last year."

"More gasps echoed around the room as people found out that the international bestselling pop star was dead. Thomas and Cat could hear people discussing about Annie, what would become of her new album and (quite bizarrely) who would be top of the charts next.

Thomas and Cat managed to make their way to the front, where some people were putting some tape around the body. She was lying on the floor, her face as pale as the piece of paper you're reading off right now. She was wearing a fur coat, made from some animal or another and a pair of high heels on her feet. Her eyes were wide open with shock like she'd just seen a ghost, and her lips smudged with lipstick were closed. But the most noticeable thing was that there was a knife sitting next to her.

A man wearing white trousers who had green spots on his tie and jacket said to himself, "Who in the world would do such a crime?"

"If I find that nefarious murderer anywhere I'm gonna knock 'im out," said a women, doing a fake karate kick and accidentally knocking herself over.

"Steady on love," said a man picking her up.

A child came wandering in. "What's going on," he said.

"This is no place for little children like you," said presumably his Mother, covering his eyes and taking him out.

"This is a disaster!" said a man from the crowd of bustling people.

"More than a disaster," said another one.

"A calamity!"

"A mishap!"

"Affliction!"

"I'll post it on Facebook!"

"Forget Facebook, Twitter!"

"Fiasco!"

"Cataclysm!"

"Tragedy!"

"Crippling!"

"Dire!"

"Another word meaning bad!"

Thomas couldn't take the noise anymore. "Shut up!" he said without thinking then, "I'll get that murderer." He'd meant to say that under his breath, but everyone still heard it. They all went back to their carriages as two men came on the train and, as it stopped, took the body of the late pop star off. As a man passed Thomas, he came close and whispered to him,

"On you mate." Then walked off.

Cat walked up to him.

"I didn't mean to do it, I mean say what I said it just sort of came out-" Thomas blurted.

"It's okay," said Cat. "It happens to everyone once in a while."

They went back to their apartments.

"Hey, wait, where's your compartment?"

"Over here," said Cat, pointing to the cabin opposite his.

"A bit of a coincidence, isn't it?" and with that, they split off to go to sleep.

Thomas couldn't get to sleep. It had been a hectic day. But he knew something. Something that no-one else saw. To him it was still a mystery, but he hoped that it would explain itself soon. He suddenly thought about his parents. *Block it out Thomas, block it out.* He thought to himself. *I'll find them one day.*

He rolled over on his side and fell to sleep.

As he lay on his bed, his mind and body shutting down, a few cabins away sat a murderer. The person was flicking through a small pad, filled with spidery handwriting.

"I will soon have it. I will."

Chapter Three
Greater Gashfield Gazette, only 50p!

The next day, Thomas woke up to the birds tweeting and singing, and the first few stray sunbeams shining through the curtains and onto his bed, filling the room with light and hope for the day ahead. Thomas got dressed, had his breakfast and brushed his teeth, then went out to see if Cat was ready. She was already sitting in her seat, in her same suit and beret, except the French hat was at a slight angle.

"Good morning," said Cat, turning around to face him. She had the sort of face that you have when you just realised that someone has just coated your door in tar. If you don't know what that expression is, it's sort of a puzzled one.

"Are you okay?" replied Thomas, who had never had his door covered in tar.

"Just thinking about the incident yesterday. Do you think there's going to be another murder?"

"I don't know. But I do know that the murderer

must be looking for an object. The contents of Annie's handbag was scattered every where."

"I was thinking that as well," said Cat nonchalantly.

"I think we should look for that object, catch the murderer and find out what the object means."

"I think we should go see if anyone else is awake," and with that, they stood up and walked to the other compartment carriages.

As Thomas walked down the aisle, he noticed the most grimy looking room he had ever seen. The door frame was as cracked and as dirty as a hard-boiled egg dropped on the ground and rolled down a dirty hill. The paint was peeling and the doormat was ripped, torn and worn out. The '1' was missing from the two digit number, so it looked like a lower number than it actually was, and one of the hinges was missing.

When Thomas was booking the tickets (his uncle was too 'busy' eating burgers to do it himself) he noticed that the specific room had been reduced down to £2.50 instead of the usual price and there were no photos of it. Thomas had no idea who would stay in it for a long journey to Montpellier.

He didn't know he would be in there soon, fighting a ruthless and despicable person.

Thomas went back to the carriage and sat down

in his seat, accidentally scraping his side on a piece of metal in the seat and hurting himself. He winced in pain and had a look at it. A fair scrape, but not too bad. He tried to ignore the pain by staring at the window. He watched the picturesque landscape fly past, as though he didn't have a care in the world. He saw the sheep gently plod their way over the hills and it reminded him of a time he and his mum and dad were going to London on the train. Thomas sat next to his mother, both of them pressing their faces at the window and watching the sheep whilst giggling. He wished he was still with his mother and father. He didn't want to think what could be happening to them at this point in time. He wondered if they had passed away yet.

He didn't want to know.

And he didn't want to know where they had gone on that fateful evening, years ago.

He blinked, almost pulling himself out of his trance and dragged his head away from the window to see Cat come and sit down next to him.

"Look at this Thomas," she said, and gave him a large bunch of papers, known as the Greater Gashfield Gazette. Thomas started to read out loud:

'MURDERER STRIKES ON TRAIN

'Last Saturday, a ruthless murderer attacked a train from London, heading to Montpellier in France. The famous

pop star Annie Red was aboard the train,when the lights flickered out and afterwards was found lying on the floor dead. The contents of her handbag was also scattered across the floor next to her. The train driver is doing everything he possibly can to keep the other passengers safe, but is refusing to cancel the journey, no matter how much the council persuade him.

"Annie Red was about to release her new album, "Under the Same Star as You" very shortly and was heading to France to fully release it... blah blah blah and... yes!

"We talked to the communications manager about this tragedy:

"Awful, it was. Such a drepressin' death, ain't it? The lights went out and I thought it were another one of those blimmin' power cuts we're havin', but the murderer must ave turned the lights out some 'ow. If 'e did, I have no idea 'ow he blimmin' did it."

Thomas put the Greater Gashfield Gazette down and turned to Cat.

"They missed something out in that report," he said.

"What?"

"That there was a knife at the scene."

A long crackle came through on the intercom speaker.

Chapter Four
An Escapee, a Hole, and Some Cats

"Ahem. Your train communications officer. We have just realised that the jail cell at the back of the train is empty. An' we put someone in it back in London. Do not panic. That is all."

There was a crackle, but you could still hear them talking.

"I mean, the blimmin' prisoner just gone an' blimmin' escaped now, ain't he? It might be that blimmin' murderer tryin' to kill everyone on my train who did it."

"Um, Mr Johnson?"

"Yeah?"

"You forgot to turn the speaker off."

"Oh, right."

Another loud crackle and the speaker turned off.

The same man in the suit with spots on stood with his arm in the air.

"So you," he said, pointing to the intercom speaker, "are telling us that we are sharing the train with an escaped criminal and a mad murderer that's trying to kill everyone, and you tell us 'That is all'? Do you think we're all gonna go 'Oh heck, now a criminal has escaped. Well, who cares?' and put my feet up again and continue reading the newspaper? No! You must be absolutely off your head to think that! I almost want to be killed by the murderer now!"

At that point the lights went out.

More screams (mainly from the ladies now) echoed around the room followed by several curses and 'It's only a power cut' to small children in distress. Eventually, after what seemed like an eternity, the lights flooded the room again.

And sure enough, the man with green spots on his tie and jacket was lying on the floor.

Dead.

A kitchen knife lay on the floor like last time.

This time there was a small note next to it. Cat picked it up and read it.

"Moro Entither," she said, a rather puzzled look on her face.

"Moro Entither? What in the world does it mean?" Thomas said.

Two policemen came running in.

"Please leave the site, we must evacuate!" one policeman said, holding a roll of police tape in his hand.

Thomas and Cat left as they were told to and went back to their seats.

Cat's hand was clenched over the note, so tight that her fingers were starting to go white.

"Well, he got what he wanted, didn't he?" Thomas said.

"Yes, unfortunately," Cat replied.

"I was thinking we should go have a look at that prison, see how the criminal escaped."

"Let's go."

Thomas and Cat went down to the carriages, past all the passengers sitting in their seats, as if waiting for something to happen. One of them shifted in his seat awkwardly and then turned around to look out of the window, despite the train being in a tunnel. Thomas and Cat walked along until they reached the driver's cabin. They stopped in their tracks as the driver came towards them, as if he knew they were about to ask him something.

"Good afternoon, Catherine and Thomas," he said, emerging from the darkness of his cabin and into the light of the bulb above them.

He was a frail old man with wrinkles covering his face. What was left of his hair on his shiny head was white and wispy. He wore a red and blue uniform, the colours of the train company.

"Are you the one who spoke to us over the

intercom?" Cat questioned him.

"No, that's the announcements person."

"Oh, okay. We were wondering if we could have a look at the prison cell."

"Yes, sure, follow me."

The old man squinted at Cat and Thomas, and gestured for them to follow him. They walked down a small and cramped passageway and reached a wall of metal.

"Where do we go now?" asked Thomas.

"Oh, I think we just…" The train driver kicked the wall of metal, and it dislodged to reveal a small tunnel.

They entered a room and saw that it was filled with cages, all stacked on top of each other. The walls had water dripping down them, and there was a large cage at the back which was empty. But the most noticeable things about the room was that there was a gaping hole in the centre, and all the cages were filled with cats.

"Um…why is there a gaping hole in the centre of the room? And I thought all the cages would be filled with prisoners, not cats," said Thomas, looking overly confused.

"Oh! There's a big hole because the builders ran out of material for the train, and the prisoner's cell is over here, ignore those cats." The train driver pointed to the large empty cage at the back. "I'll leave you to look around for a bit and then come back."

Thomas and Cat walked around the cages. The train driver had given them a pair of keys so that they could around the inside of the cell.

Cat opened the door to find that there was food and water all over the floor. The whole floor was made out of sheets of metal, that vibrated as the train rattled along the track.

Thomas and Cat walked around for a while, inspecting and closely looking at everything that was worth inspecting and closely looking at.

Thomas was closely inspecting a slice of bacon quiche in the corner of the room, when he dragged his leg back and one of the metal sheets came loose.

"Cat," he said. "Come and have a look at this."

"Looks like we found how the prisoner escaped then," Cat said with her hands on her hips staring down into the hole, which was just big enough for a slim person to climb down.

Underneath the train, a man hauled himself past a large pipe protruding from the underside of the carriage. He narrowly dodged another one, whilst thinking to himself, *I must get away now, before they blame me for all those murders that have been going on.*

He could just about hear, above the clickety clack

of the train, footsteps of people above him.

He finally reached the end of the train.

He prepared himself, making sure that he wouldn't hurt any of his limbs when he dropped.

He took three deep breaths and let go.

It had all gone as planned.

The train rumbled over him as he lay between the tracks. He then rolled out and ran off into the distance.

"Kay, 'ave ya 'ad enough ov yer dilly dallyin' around," said the announcer, coming into the room via the secret hatch.

"Yes, thank you. But you're the announcer, not the train driver aren't you?" said Cat

"Well that blimmin' train driver's got a blimmin' train to drive, use yer brain!"

"Oh. Sorry. Yes, we are finished now thank you."

"This way then," he said, pointing to the secret hatch. "I'll take those keys as well, thank yer."

They crawled through it, and headed back to find that it had gone dark.

"See you in the morning," said Thomas.

Chapter Five
The Breakdown

It was morning. Thomas woke up, got dressed and had breakfast as quick as he could.

He knew who the murderer was. And he was going to prove it today.

He ran down to the carriage. He needed to get everything prepared.

White board and white board pen, umbrella, ID card and finally, the proof.

Everyone flooded into the room. Even the train driver.

"I'll get straight to the point then, shall I?" said Thomas. "I'll explain why and how I know later, but first I will tell you who it is. Out of everyone on the train, the murderer is—"

"You're right," said a sneering voice, "but you didn't realise what trouble and hassle you got yourself into finding that out."

Thomas felt a wave of nausea hit him, and he felt two hands hit him as he fell onto the cold, metal floor. The screams and shouts seemed distant. He heard Cat shout something, but he couldn't hear what.

He couldn't move. He was way too tired to get out of the way.

It was too late.

His mother and father were there again in his head, saying the last words he would ever hear them say.

"Thomas," his mother was saying.

"Yes?" Thomas replied.

"Me and your dad are just going out for a while, so you are going to stay here with your uncle."

"No! Not my uncle!"

"Yes, and don't be rude."

And then they were gone, fading away.

And Thomas was gone too.

Thomas woke up sweating. He'd had a nightmare. It was still dark outside.

He checked his wristwatch, laid out on the bedside table next to him. It showed 3 am.

He rolled over on his side, and fell back to sleep.

When Thomas woke up for the second time he went to see Cat. Everyone was getting up and going to their seats in the seating carriage.

"Hi Cat," Thomas said, as Cat came out of her room.

"Hello."

Suddenly there was a loud shriek from one of the other carriages.

"Bill Disrod! He's dead!"

Thomas and Cat ran over to the crime scene and as expected Bill Disrod was lying on the floor in the same setup as the previous murders. The kitchen knife, the contents of his bag scattered across the floor and a small slip of paper.

Thomas picked up this piece of paper and read it out loud.

"C.M.C. That's what it says. C.M.C."

"I've heard that before," said a man, wearing plaid shorts and leaning over Thomas's shoulder.

"I mean there's a shop called 'Cut and Mended Clothes', but I'm sure the murderer wouldn't put the name of his favourite tailors when he has just killed three people, would he?" said Cat, joining in the conversation.

"No, he most likely wouldn't," said Thomas.

It turned out that Bill Disrod was an old man who went to London to visit his cousin, Hester, and was heading back over to Montpellier.

Thomas and Cat went back to their seats and started to talk, whilst gazing aimlessly out of the window.

"Where do your parents live, Cat?" Thomas said,

starting a conversation.

"Oh, they travel around the world. I think they're at some exotic place at the moment or something."

"They don't take you on holidays?"

"But they say, 'It's not a holiday, it's for work, Cat.'"

"Oh, what's their job then?"

"I don't rightly know. I heard a conversation between them a couple of years ago, it was something about a shop or a building, but then they came out and ushered me back to bed. What happened to your mother, Thomas? I saw your father on the station platform but I didn't see your mother."

"Oh, that was my uncle on the platform. I despise him. My mother and father went missing a couple of years ago, but I have no idea where they went."

"That's… sad."

"I know, everyone says that when I tell them. But anyway, I had this really weird dream last night . . ."

Thomas went on to tell Cat how the dream went and she looked shocked.

"Crikey!" she said. "That's one heck of a dream."

"It might be a warning or some—"

The lights flickered out and the train stopped.

"It's another murder!" someone shouted. "Everyone save yourselves!"

The intercom speaker crackled into life.

"Everyone please go ta the exit door by the seatin' carriage."

Thomas and Cat went outside along with the flow of people, and the man was standing outside holding a wad of paper. The station was just up the track and so he led them there.

"ALRIGHT!" he said with a booming voice. "THE BLIMMIN' TRAIN 'AS JUST 'AD A BREAKDOWN, SO YA ALL ALLOWED TO DILLY DALLY A BIT, BUT REPORT RIGHT BACK 'ERE AT EIGHT O CLOCK. UNLESS YA WANNA WALK TO Montpellier."

Nobody looked keen to walk.

"Kay, everyone, I gotta make sure ya all 'ere, so I'm gonna go through the list of passengers, kay? Annie Red?"

"Dead, sir."

"Bret Selvil?"

"Dead, sir."

"Bill Disrod?"

"Dead, sir."

"Bob Dandly?"

"Here, sir," said a small voice from the back of the crowd.

"Catherine Merillin?"

"Here, sir."

This continued on to the last person on the train.

"Ya can all go now," he said, shaking his hand for them to go away.

"Where should we go?" said Thomas.

"How long do we have?" Cat asked.

"Well, it's three o'clock at the moment, so we've got five hours."

It was a picturesque afternoon in France, as people were in the hot, stuffy and beautiful conditions. Some people were walking through the decadent archways on posh buildings, some just wandering around without a care in the world. Houses lined the streets with people walking in and out of them.

"Let's go to the shopping mall," said Thomas suddenly. "I want to look for Cut and Mended Clothes."

"Okay, the nearest one I know is in the 'La Liberte' that's just around the corner."

Thomas and Cat walked just around the corner to find that the shopping mall was sitting in the middle of a dilapidated part of France. It looked quite out of place, as it was a large fancy building but surrounded by run down industrial buildings.

Thomas and Cat walked into the building and found that it had a stunning interior. Long, elegant patterns flowed across the smooth marble floor, while tall glass statues of dolphins could be seen spitting water into a large bowl on the floor, surrounded by benches.

Thomas had a look around. The shops were ordered A-Z and included a large variety of shops, like Betty's Boutique; Frank's Flowers; Gethin's Groceries; Lillie's Lamborghini's; Latin Lessons with Luther; Jack's Jaunty Jibs and Quirells's Quadruple Quagmire Quailing Quadrants of Querulous Queer Querns.

"Where do you want to go?" Cat said.

"I don't know, but I'd like to see how many customers that shop gets," Thomas said, pointing to Quirells's Quadruple Quagmire Quailing Quadrants of Querulous Queer Querns.

Thomas and Cat wound up wandering aimlessly around the endless web of paths and corridors, coming back several times to the same spot they started in.

They were wandering past Jack's Jaunty Jibs when Cat spotted a set of steps at one end of the hall.

"Thomas," she said, nudging him and pointing to the steps. "That's where Cut and Mended Clothes is."

"I'm not really interested in tailors."

"I mean to have a look around for any clues

about C.M.C., not get you a new jumper fitted."

"Oh."

A man started to walk towards them, holding a big bulky camera.

"No one goes in that darn place anymore son," he said, whilst lowering his camera. He had a large, bushy beard, which concerned Thomas and Cat as they couldn't see much of his face. All they could see were deep, icy eyes.

"You'd be crazy to go in that place," he said. "Some people think it's cursed. And that darn shop keeper has been alive forever."

Thomas and Cat walked slowly off, and the man just stood there and watched them go, one eye twitching slowly.

Chapter Six
Cut and Mended Clothes

Thomas and Cat hurried down the steps. They turned into a long passageway, which had lots of rubbish chutes poking out of the wall, which explained the black bags on the floor that Thomas and Cat had to clamber over. Eventually they reached Cut and Mended Clothes, and saw that it was a shop that had not been built very well. It had once had a neon sign but it was so caked in dirt you could hardly see it. The wall was painted beige, but the paint was peeling and was more a grey colour now. The bricks were also falling out leaving the inside more of the outside.

Thomas and Cat walked inside and, to their dismay, it was as bad as the outside. The interior consisted of a concrete floor, half chipped away, several tipped up wardrobes and a few filing cabinets, one of which was overflowing with measuring tapes. Behind a cracked mahogany desk sat a wild haired man slumped over a pile of papers falling from the desk and onto the floor. A pot of pens sat next to him.

As Thomas and Cat entered the derelict and devastated building, the man at the desk shot up, his eyes wide.

"Afternoon," he said with a strong Cockney accent. "Welcome ta Cut and Mend . . ." But he never finished his sentence as he fall back to sleep and began snoring loudly.

"I guess we're allowed to look around then," Cat said.

They walked through a stained white door and into a back room filled with boxes packed with clothes. Thomas went over to a large pile of the boxes and began ripping them open.

"Hmm," he said, as he rifled through the boxes. "Over sized raincoat, two-piece suit, three-piece suit, nope, nothing here."

But then he pulled some boxes out of the way and there sat a large wooden trapdoor.

"I wonder what kind of shop would keep a trapdoor in the back room?"

"Let's find out."

Thomas and Cat opened the slab of wood, to find that it lead to a ladder going a short way down. They clambered down through a claustrophobic passage and found themselves in a cellar, thick with rubble and dust.

"It looks like a wine cellar, but the wine boxes are stacked up in that corner over there," Thomas said, pointing.

They headed over and started to haul the boxes into another pile in the centre of the room. Eventually they had finished and Thomas noticed a large wooden door behind the boxes.

"Look at that, it looks like it's from Victorian times," said Cat.

But Thomas wasn't looking at the door, he continued to stare, rather puzzled, at the floor where a piece of paper lay with the letters C.M.C. on it.

"C.M.C., what does that mean?" Thomas said.

"But look here," Cat said, taking the papers off Thomas, "it says: 'Scarlet will board the train on Christmas Eve, as the ticket master finishes his job and leaves. She will quickly change out of her cleaners uniform and leave her cap and broomstick behind the building on the far right and then quickly catch the train as it leaves the platform. She will slowly murder all the passengers until she finds the object. She will stay in the only available room, Room th—' and the rest is just too illegible to read."

Thomas looked at the folder.

"The rest of it is missing. It looks like it was burnt off."

"Do you think we should take a look through

there, Thomas?" Cat said, pointing at the door.

Thomas didn't need to say anything, because Cat had already walked up to the door. She pushed it open and Thomas followed her up the cracked stone steps where she pushed open another door, causing an avalanche of rubble and dust to fall in front of them.

"Darn it!" said Cat, as she looked in dismay at her clothes, which were now nearly as dusty as the room itself.

"Come on, let's go have a look at this room," said Thomas, impatiently.

They walked inside to find it was an old Victorian reception area. It was covered in ash, and some of the wooden ceiling had collapsed, like someone had jumped straight through the floor above them. There was a desk at the front of the room with a large pin board above it.

"Wow," said Thomas, "it looks like it was from Victorian times."

"And there was a fire," Cat said. They stood there for a while, gazing in wonderment at the oldest place they had ever seen.

They were standing so still they could even hear the footsteps of three men run into the shop above.

Chapter Seven
A Man and His Phone Call

Meanwhile a man walked casually down a street in London, thinking to himself.

"Think I got the best job ever, making phonecalls in secret, eh dog?" he thought as he looked at a small and lost Shih Tzu cross the road.

He was a tall man with a bald head and a broad smile crossing his squashed face. He slipped his hand in his top jacket pocket inside his coat as he reached the only red telephone box in his town. He pulled out a tiny slip of paper on which he scribbled down a number that he had had received from his boss over the phone, 368951. He put the slip of paper down on the telephone directory and started to dial the number.

He was halfway through when he heard a noise. It sounded like a clunking against the glass. He looked up and saw that a few teenagers were chucking stones at the window pane of the tele-phone box, laughing. He looked sternly at them and they ran off. He finished dialling the number.

"Stupid kids," he said quietly to himself as the phone was ringing.

"Hello?" said a voice on the other end.

"Can I speak to your announcement man please?"

"Yes, umm, may I ask why?"

"Oh, it's just a friend to tell him a few things that he needs to know."

"Okay, I'll just pass you on."

There was the sound of footsteps and then muttering, then the phone crackled and voice spoke.

"'ello?"

"It's Pete. I was just calling to say that I've just got married to a wonderful girl called Sue, and wanted you to know that we're going on honeymoon, and so I won't be back tomorrow."

This was C.M.C.'s secret code whenever they wanted to talk to someone about business.

"What's 'e told ya to tell me this time then, eh?" he said, his voice quieter this time.

"He said to tell you to get rid of the children called Thomas and Cat, because they're on to us. He said if you don't do as he tells you, you will follow in C.'S footsteps."

"Kay. Did he say anyfin' else 'bout work or not?"

"Nope. Okay, I'll see you after our honeymoon,

and I assure you, she's very nice."

He slammed down the phone and walked out of the box, an even larger smile on his face than before.

Chapter Eight
A Run Through France

Thomas and Cat looked at each other in panic, as they heard the footsteps above.

"We need to get out of here, and rather quick," Cat said, rather dramatically.

Upstairs, three men entered the building.

"Johnson," the middle man said to a short man, "you check the filing cabinet and clothes rack. Dominic, check the cellar and I'll interrogate the man."

The three men ran off to do their duties.

As the middle man tried to interrogate the man at the desk (but he wouldn't wake up), Dominic ran down into the cellar just as Thomas and Cat clambered up the hole. He ran over to them.

"Do you have those files?" he scowled.

Thomas looked at Cat as he silently slipped the files into her hands.

"Umm, no, I don't know what you're talking about," Cat said.

"I know you're lying, just let me see your hands."

Cat opened up her hands and showed him that they were empty.

"And yours, boy," the man said to Thomas.

Cat put her hands behind her back as Thomas silently slipped her the files again and then showed his hands empty.

"Grr, you don't have them."

He walked off and spotted the ladder. He clambered down and just as he had got to the bottom, Cat kicked the trapdoor over and Thomas locked it.

They ran up the steps just as the main man came down to find Dominic.

He saw that Dominic wasn't there and that two children stood in his way.

"Excuse me," he said, and then, "Hey! Come back here!" as he saw the papers behind Cat's back. Thomas and Cat were already out of the door and running out of the building.

You know when you get to that really good part of your book when there is a chase? And you sit rigid on the edge of your seat, your face going pale and then your mother calls you that it's time for tea, but you can't put the book down, like someone's put superglue on your hands? But then the chase finishes and you realise that it's lasagna for tea? This chase is nothing like that. Sorry.

The main man ran up the steps, and when

Johnson saw him running he joined in too. Thomas and Cat were already running up the narrow alley, carefully stepping over the bin bags. They made their way up the steps and into the main shopping mall hall, with the two men following closely behind them.

And that's when Cat noticed the other wiritng, the only other writing that was readable.

Meanwhile, Dominic was in a bit of a sticky situation. He sat on the floor, a large bump on his head. He looked up at the locked trapdoor.

Those kids!

He lowered his head and then heard his phone ring. He stood up, shook the dust off his clothes and took the phone out of his pocket.

"Hello?"

"Where are you?" said the unmistakable voice of his wife. "I told you to be back by four thirty, but it's now four fifty-six! Tea's gone cold now!"

"Sorry, Jane, I got caught up in a bit of business, and I'm sort of looki—"

"Okay, fine! Bye!"

The phone went dead.

He looked at his watch.

"Yep, it's exactly four fifty-six," he said to himself. "Darn it, it was lasagna for tea tonight, too."

Thomas and Cat were running past Quirells's Quadruple Quagmire Quailing Quadrants of Querulous Queer Querns when Cat turned to Thomas.

"There's a tiny bit more writing here, Thomas," she said. "It says, 'Scarlet will need to find the—'" Cat tripped over someone's leg as they stuck it out as some kind of prank.

Cat hit the floor face first. The papers flew out of her hands and she quickly scrambled to get up. She ran off with Thomas, and the two men stopped chasing her. The main man picked up the papers and the other one continued chasing Cat and Thomas.

They ran through the sliding doors outside, narrowly dodging a cyclist who rode into the shopping mall. They headed down the street, the man hot on their heels, and swerved around several people and various bins placed carelessly in odd places on the pavement. The train station came into view around the corner, and Thomas and Cat ran up to it. They pushed past people as they saw their train was about to start moving.

That was when a newspaper seller bundled into them.

"Eh, ya wanna buy The Big Issue, do ya?"

"No, sorry sir," said Cat. "Our train has just started to move."

"It got a lot of news about Annie Red." He looked up. Thomas and Cat weren't standing in front of him anymore, as they had run to catch their moving train.

"Where the divil they gone?" he said, looking around.

Meanwhile, Thomas and Cate were running alongside the track, just as the train started to speed up.

Thomas looked at Cat.

Then they jumped.

They landed on the very edge of the small platform on the train, with the words PLEASE MIND THE GAP printed in broad yellow lettering in front of them. They stood for a moment, the wind blowing in their faces, half hanging out over the ground rushing by them at around 85mph. Then Thomas hit the button on the outside of the door and they climbed inside.

A woman was sitting close to the door and shrieked rather loudly as they came in.

"Some young thieves have boarded the train!" she shrieked and dropped her handbag on the floor.

"We're not thieves!" said Cat. "We're passengers."

"Oh yes, I'm sorry, I recognise you now," she said, blushed and hurried off to her room.

Thomas and Cat hurried off down the aisle and went to Cat's room.

"Do you have a notebook we could write down all the information in?"

"Yes, in fact I do," Cat replied. From her pocket she pulled out a rather attractive notebook with a bright yellow glossy cover. She flicked past various notes and labelled diagrams until she found a free page.

"Okay," said Thomas. "So we know that the murderer is called Scarlet, that she is looking for an object and that she's staying in a room with a number beginning with 'thir—'"

Cat was scribbling down the information so furiously that her pen dug into the paper and drew a long tear across the page. Thomas glanced over to see what had happened. Through the rip he could just make out the words: 'They're gone. I can't believe they followed the letter. Ja—' There was more but Cat had been quick to flip the page over.

"It used to be my grandmother's," she said.

"I think we should ask the announcements man if we can have his list of people on the train, and then we can see which room Scarlet is in." But Thomas didn't even need an answer as Cat had already stood up and was walking out of the door.

NOT A CHAPTER

As you saw from the title of the chapter, this is not a chapter.

This is definitely not a chapter.

I decided to put this chapter-that-is-not-a-chapter in here for two reasons. First of all to inform you about something. And second of all to annoy you, because you want to find out what happens next, but I have put this in so you have to read through it all.

But I would like to introduce you to two odd characters with two odd names. They will appear in the next book.

They are called Pope and Smike.

Yes, I know, you think it should be Pipe and Smoke, but no, it's Pope and Smike.

They are detectives, and are related to the next scene that happens. You won't see why, unless you read the second book in the series, (which hasn't been written yet, so don't go trying to buy it off Amazon).

THAT WAS NOT A CHAPTER SO YOU SHOULD HAVE JUST IGNORED IT. ALWAYS IGNORE CHAPTERS-WHICH-ARE-NOT-ACTUALLY-CHAPTERS.

Chapter Ten
Into the Hovel

The announcement man picked up a cigarette lying on the table and popped the end into his mouth. He opened the bottom drawer of a small filing cabinet and pulled out a red cigarette lighter. He flicked the switch on the side and a flame burst into life on top of it. He lit the end of the cigarette.

Just at that moment a knock sounded on the mahogany door. He jumped up, dropping the cigarette and burning his finger. The cigarette fell on the floor and he stamped on it and twisted his foot, grinding the tobacco into the the thin layer of the carpet.

There was a rap of knuckles on the door again.

"I'm coming," he said through gritted teeth, running over to the cabinet drawer and pulling out a cloth. He started to scrub furiously at the black mark, but the chances of a clean carpet were futile. He dropped the cloth over the mark to cover it and opened the door.

"Hello," said Cat. "We were wondering if we

could borrow a list of the passengers on the train."

"Ah, um, I can't lend you mine, 'cos I use it all the time, but I expect ya could borrow one of the cleaner's ones, eh?"

"Yes, please, but where's the cleaner's room?"

"Look, I'll show ya, eh?"

They walked out of the door, the man leading the way. Eventually he reached the back of the train where the secret hatch was. He kicked the panel next to it, revealing a passage with a door at the end of it. He opened the door with a key and Thomas and Cat entered the pitch black room.

The man pushed them further in and then shut and locked the door behind them.

"Hey! Is there a light switch in here?" said Cat.

"Yes," said a voice. "But we don't know where it is."

Cat leaned against a wall. "You mean to say we are stuck in a pitch black room with no means of escape?"

The back her head head hit the wall in annoyance, and the room filled with light.

"She's found the light switch!" said a small, Chinese man.

The room had metal walls, and some hammocks in one corner, some buckets and mops in another.

Thomas and Cat turned to face a girl, who was

small, the height of a ten-year-old, but she looked to be in her twenties. She wore a dark green jumpsuit, just like all the others. Her hair was tied in a bun.

They could see some of the other people in the room, and they were all the same size, and the same age. Except for the small Chinese boy. He had a broad smile on his face, quite happy from the light that Cat had accidentally discovered when she hit the hidden light switch. He wore a pair of overalls, with the legs rolled up to knee height.

Thomas and Cat turned back to Lola. (Have I told you already that she was called Lola?)

"We'd like to ask a favour of you, actually two favours," Cat said.

"Hello. My name is Lola. What is your names?"

"Umm, actually, it's 'What are your names,' not 'What is your names.'"

"I do not understand what you is saying."

"Never mind, I'm Thomas and this is Cat."

"Do you mind," said Cat, "if we borrow your list of passengers aboard this train?"

"Hmm, next question?"

"And how do we get out of here?"

"Two questions, two answers I shall give. Question one."

"You know, you don't have to do it like a quiz

show," Thomas said.

"I practice for when I am older. I be a quiz master."

"Oh, sorry."

"As I is saying, question one, can we borrow a list of passengers on the train? Answer, yes. Here, take mine, I never use it anyway. One point awarded for anyone who got the answer. Question two, how do we get out of here? Answer, through here."

She pulled up a loose sheet of metal from the underside of the train.

"Why do you never use it, Lola?"

"Oh, too scary. And then we would never get any money, homes or food."

"Fair enough."

Thomas and Cat climbed down in the hole as Lola put the piece back.

"And don't forget to award yourself a point if you get the answer correct!" she said loudly as the sheet of metal covered their entrance.

Chapter Eleven
The Pot of Tipp-ex

Meanwhile, a man wedged himself between two walls. He shoved his hand in his pocket, rummaging around, then pulled out a pot of Tipp-Ex.

"Come on," he thought, "this needs to work."

He shook the pot feebly, it was hard to shake in a small space. He pulled the cap off with his teeth, then threw the pot onto the floor. It rolled, then fell down a drain.

The man cursed silently, then pulled out a microphone.

"Jasmine!" he hissed into it. "It didn't work!"

"I see them Zain. Run, Zain, you need to run! They're after you!"

Have you ever wanted to see all the mechanical parts of something? Like taking apart a computer or dismantling a record player? Well, it was the same for Thomas, and his needs were satisfied when he crawled under the train. It was a big, black mess of pipes and gears, pulleys, valves, pistons, levers, cogs, gauges, couplets and springs. They narrowly dodged a large, protruding pipe from the sheet of metal on the bottom of the train.

"Phew, nearly there, I can see the hole in the prison floor from here," Thomas said.

"Good, my arms are really aching.

"Hey, wait! The train is going around a corner! Brace yourself!"

And sure enough the trains was heading for a corner. It flew around the corner so quickly in fact that Thomas and Cat went flying off the underside of the train, like toy dolls.

The man did as Jasmine told him to.

He ran.

He ran as fast as he could, past famous buildings and up through streets, lanes, avenues and alleys, boulevards and back streets. He eventually ran up a cul-de-sac called Rue de la Colline, to find that it ended in a few houses set in a circular fashion around the bottom of the road. A dead end.

He could just make out the distant figures of his enemies down the cul-de-sac from him. He didn't have much time to escape.

Suddenly he spotted a large fence set against a bush. He ran over to it and under cover of the large bush he hauled himself over the fence, landing on a railway track. He ran down the track and across the other side.

He'd just got to the opposite side of the track when some papers flew out of his pocket.

"Jasmine!" he hissed into the microphone as he walked up to a platform. "I'm there."

"Good, Zain. Head to the building and give the papers to N."

You probably don't need me to explain what happened when Z. arrived to give the papers to N. and how angry that J. was when she found out that Z. had dropped the papers, and therefore couldn't tell G. go give them to P. for examination by H. which then got very complicated and I'm not going to waste your time going into all the details about what happened.

Instead, I think we should head back to Thomas and Cat.

Chapter Twelve
A Small Scrap Of Rubbish

Thomas and Cat rolled across the floor of the track and out into the open air. The train finished its turn around the corner and disappeared from view.

Thomas looked at Cat. "The train's gone, Cat. Our train's left us."

But Cat was interested in other things. She could see some papers poking out from behind a bush, just neatly tucked away like they had been placed there. Thomas noticed Cat looking at it.

"Come on, Cat, stop staring at a piece of rubbish, we need to catch our train before it reaches the next stop."

"Thomas, look at this," she said, picking up the pile of notes. "It says C.M.C. at the top."

And sure enough the letters were printed in the same broad lettering as the papers they found.

Thomas started to read.

"—anagram. Esme should have the object soon. Be warned though, she is the great granddaughter of Scarlet, the girl who caused all that trouble. We've found that she will kill in alphabetical order, and slowly reveal clues on slips of paper as stated above. We do not yet know which room she is sleeping in, but we presume room th—"

"We need to get back to the train now, and we can look at our discoveries there."

They walked up to the platform and then into the bustling city.

"Excuse me," said Cat to a thin taxi driver with old spidery fingers. "Can you take us to Junction des Crimes Penalement Maitris?" Her French accent was perfect.

"Hop dans le dos, que je vais vous y emmene gratuitment, enfants bas age."

Neither of them understood, but by the smile painted across his face, and his small hand gesture to the back door, they guessed they were allowed to travel free.

Halfway down the road he started to talk a lot of nonsense.

"Avez-vous entendu parler que nouveaux scientifiques de machine fangled ont concocte avec vous faire voler?"

By the time he'd finished his sentence they were at the station, and just in time because the train had arrived too. They asked the driver to stop where he was and got out.

"Non dimenticate di acquistare la vostra machina!" he said as they ran up the platform toward the train.

Back on board, Thomas and Cat consulted their discoveries for the second time.

"Now we know that we are not looking for a Scarlet, but for an Esme," said Cat.

Well, if we get out that list of passenger names we might be able to work out which room this Esme is in."

"Let's have a look." Cat pulled out the list of passengers. "It says that the room begins with Thir—, so there can only be eleven rooms. Room Thirteen, vacant, Room Thirty, vacant, Room Thirty-one Bill Disrod, he's dead . . ."

This continued until there was only one room left, but that was Annie Red's room.

"Then we don't know," said Thomas. There's three rooms vacant, Thirteen, Thirty and Thirty-six. Esme could be in any one of those!"

I'm sure you know what dramatic irony is. When the audience has a fuller knowledge of what is happening in the story than the characters do. As I have already mentioned and described Room Thirteen, you will probably guess that the murderer is in Room Thirteen. And from dramatic irony, you can probably guess that as soon as Thomas says, "I hope there won't be any more murders before we work out where the murderer is staying," a murder will happen.

"I hope there won't be any more murders before we work out where the murderer is staying," Thomas said.

As if on cue, the lights flickered out. Several screams echoed in the carriages and then, after what seemed like ages, the lights flickered back on.

A woman screamed again.

"Shriek!" She fell down on her knees and burst into tears. "My husband never did anything to hurt anyone! He never would hurt anyone. He never even did anything bad. Apart from robbing that bank. Allegedly."

She burst into tears again.

The train stopped and the doors opened. The three same policemen came running in and dragged the body off.

That was when Thomas noticed the small slip of paper floating down from above them. He picked it up.

"Anagram," he said.

"What was that?" said Cat.

"Anagram," repeated Thomas. "Moro Entither, it must be an anagram."

Chapter Thirteen
Room Thirteen

If yuo hvae eerv atmpteedt to uesrnclamb an agan-mra, yuo wlil fdin tath it cna semsiomet be qtiut pigrxpele ot svleo.

But the one Thomas and Cat were trying to solve seemed impossible.

They came up with a few solutions.

Moor Henriett.

Ormo Teethrint. Which sounds like some sort of Asian dentist's mouth wash, which cars would use.

They could not work out for the life of them what it could be, but they knew it was not going to be an unauthorised ghastly car mouth wash.

This work carried on until dark, when they split up and went to their separate rooms.

Cat lay on her bed restlessly. She couldn't get to sleep. It was too hot. Thoughts were running through her mind like a tape recorder stuck on repeat.

The files. Esme. The murders. The rooms. Everything was just one big cobweb of mystery and murder, and they had become entangled in it by fate.

Fate, yes that was how it had happened. Fate.

"Wait!" she thought. "Fate, that's it!"

There was a flash of lightning outside, lighting up the room momentarily. Cat pulled back her duvet, pushed on her slippers, ran out of her room and knocked on Thomas' door.

It opened a few seconds later.

"Thomas!" Cat said.

"What? It's late and I'm tired."

"Thomas, I've worked out which room the killer is in."

"What? You know it?"

"Yes. Well, at least I think I know it. Room Thirteen, a suitable room for a killer. And the cheapest as well."

"Hmm, I see what you're saying. But we still don't know what the anagram is, and we can't go into the killer's room until we have a fully conceived and foolproof plan to apprehend the murderer."

Cat wasn't listening much, only really half listening. She was looking at the anagram.

"Moro, that will spell room. And entither, thirteen. We're right!"

"Okay then. Have you checked the list of passengers to see if it's vacant?"

"It is vacant."

"Oh."

"We need a plan. What are we going to do?"

I think we'll go away now and let them discuss the plan, and other things (which I cannot mention) and come back the next day, when they realise something important.

The next day, Thomas and Cat woke up fully dressed and slumped over two A4 sheets of paper. They had concocted a plan to capture the criminal. But, although they didn't know it then, their plan would be spoilt and messed up by an evil person.

They yawned quite loudly, and looked out of the window to see what kind of morning it was.

It was a quiet day, the February wind outside howling silently whilst the autumn trees shed their leaves.

They stood up lazily.

"Hey, Thomas," Cat said. "I'm gonna have a look in the passenger book."

"That's part of the plan, isn't it? See who is next to be murdered and prevent it."

"Yeah. That's part one."

She flicked open the small pad, and found a large list of names in alphabetical order. She started to read them out loud.

"Okay, here we go.

"Annie Red (Exclusive VIP, good for advertising.)

"Bill Disrod.

"Brett Sevil.

"Bob Dandly."

As she read the next name she gasped, her face turned pale and she stumbled back onto the large settee by one of the walls of the room.

"Catherine Merellin."

Thomas looked shocked. Cat was the next one to be murdered. The plan would have to be scrapped. They needed to go to Room Thirteen.

Looking at each other, they both knew what to do. They left their room, ran down the corridor to Room Thirteen and went inside.

The room was as disgusting as the door. If possible, worse. The floor was cracked and squeaked wherever you walked on it. The furniture was more a large pile of dusty wood than furniture, the curtains were more ragged than a pair of beggar's trousers that had gone through a food blender and more stained than shingles covered in tar. Thomas thought they might have been green originally.Esme turned to face them. She was wearing a leather jacket, the sort people wear for riding motorcycles, and her gloved hands gingerly touched her blond hair tied back in a bun.

"So," she said, "have you not learnt etiquette, yet? To knock the door before you enter?" She laughed. "Oh, you're next in line to be killed, aren't you Catherine? Well, I might as well get the job done now. You do know why I am doing this, don't you? To get the object my dear great grandmother Scarlet wanted. And this is the first part, to get the files. Now hand them over before I kill you."

And she produced a large knife from her pocket

"Give it to me now!"

"I - I - I don't have it!" said Cat.

"Let me check."

"Go on then."

Esme searched Cat's pockets and her handbag, but the file was nowhere to be seen

"See?" said Thomas.

"Wait, there is one more place to check."

Esme lifted Cat's French hat and the papers fell out. Esme snatched them up off the floor.

"What?" said Thomas. "How did they get there?"

They looked at each other. How had they not noticed someone shove the papers into a hat that Cat had been wearing the entire time?

They turned to notice Esme fly towards the window, smash through it and run off.

END OF BOOK ONE

I would like to mention that I have put in several Easter Eggs (as the young whippersnappers of today call it). Some of which only a few people will get, and some of which no one will get.

Here's a clue for one of them: Translate all the French in this book into English, (or translate all the English in this book into French if you want) and discover an astonishing secret.

Bonsoir, et soit dit en passant ce livre a ete ecrit sur une macine a ecrire.

Hyn yw Cymru.

Acknowledgements

I always find the acknowledgements in the back of books really boring, so I decided the make mine a bit more interesting.

These acknowledgements, are written in Cat language.

Purrrrr, purrrr meow meow purrrrr. Pur, purrrrrrrrrrr meow Robert meow Bethan purrrrrrr. Meow meow meow, Hissssss Purr *Puuurrrr*. Meow meow meow, mew mew Ken Preston purrr meow hisssss.

Meow meow mew mew mewww purrrr Matthew Preston mwa Jo Preston pur meow meoww hisss.

Meow mew, puuurr mew mow puuurrr hissssss *meowwww*.

Translated by: Lily and Luther.

About the Author

Jack Preston is eleven years old and lives in the UK. He writes books in his spare time, on a typewriter and usually with a cat on top of his bed. His hobbies are conjuring and cardistry, writing and collecting leaflets

This is his second book, and the first to be published in paperback.

Printed in Great Britain
by Amazon